HEiDi HECKELBECK

and the Never-Ending Day

By Wanda Coven
Illustrated by Priscilla Burris

LITTLE SIMON
New York London Toronto Sydney New Delhi

LITTLE SIMON
An imprint of Simon & Schuster Children's Publishing Division
1230 Avenue of the Americas, New York, New York 10020
First Little Simon hardcover edition September 2017
Copyright © 2017 by Simon & Schuster, Inc.
Also available in a Little Simon paperback edition.
All rights reserved, including the right of reproduction in whole or in part in any form. LITTLE SIMON is a registered trademark of Simon & Schuster, Inc., and associated colophon is a trademark of Simon & Schuster, Inc. For information about special discounts for bulk purchases, please contact Simon & Schuster Special Sales at 1-866-506-1949 or business@simonandschuster.com.The Simon & Schuster Speakers Bureau can bring authors to your live event. For more information or to book an event contact the Simon & Schuster Speakers Bureau at 1-866-248-3049 or visit our website at www.simonspeakers.com.
Designed by Ciara Gay
Manufactured in the United States of America 0817 FFG
10 9 8 7 6 5 4 3 2 1
Library of Congress Cataloging-in-Publication Data
Names: Coven, Wanda, author. | Burris, Priscilla, illustrator.
Title: Heidi Heckelbeck and the never-ending day / by Wanda Coven ; illustrated by Priscilla Burris. Description: First Little Simon paperback edition. | New York : Little Simon, 2017. | Series: Heidi Heckelbeck ; 21 | Summary: When Heidi experiences the perfect day she decides to sneak in a little magic to make every day just as awesome, but her plan goes awry when she relives the same perfect day over and over again. | Identifiers: LCCN 2016054406 | ISBN 9781481495240 (paperback) | ISBN 9781481495257 (hc) | ISBN 9781481495264 (eBook) | Subjects: | CYAC: Days—Fiction. | Magic—Fiction. | Witches—Fiction. | BISAC: JUVENILE FICTION / Fantasy & Magic. | JUVENILE FICTION / Imagination & Play. | JUVENILE FICTION / Readers / Chapter Books. | Classification: LCC PZ7.C83393 Hbn 2017 | DDC [Fic]—dc23
LC record available at https://lccn.loc.gov/2016054406

CONTENTS

SCRUM-DiDDLY-UMPTiOUS

Fee-bee!

Heidi opened one eye.

FEE-bee!

Heidi opened her other eye and peeked out her bedroom window.

Feeee-bee!

A chickadee hopped along a thin

branch and gave Heidi a curious look.
It had white cheeks, a white under-
belly, and a tiny black cap and bib.

Fee-bee! the bird called again.

Heidi giggled. "Hey! My name isn't
Phoebe," she whispered to the bird.
"It's Heidi."

The chickadee tilted its head and hopped to another sunny branch. Last night's thunderstorm had passed, and it was a beautiful day.

Heidi pulled her covers up to her chin. She took a deep breath in. *Mmmm,* she said to herself. *Something smells like cinnamon and spice.* She got

up on one elbow. *Dad must be making pumpkin chocolate chip muffins! And THAT means it's SATURDAY!*

A whoosh of happiness swept over Heidi. Pumpkin chocolate chip muffins were her *favorite*.

She hopped out of bed and pulled on her brand-new owl T-shirt. She

tugged on her striped tights, jean skirt, and sneakers. Then Heidi stood in front of the mirror with one hand on her hip.

"Best outfit ever!" Heidi declared happily. And then she bounded downstairs to the kitchen.

Dad greeted her in a blue-and-white-checked apron.

"Welcome to Dad's Diner!" he said, and he set a pumpkin muffin on a miniature cupcake stand in front of her.

Heidi unfolded her napkin and placed it on her lap. Then she sank her fork into the tender muffin and slid a pumpkiny, chocolaty bite into her mouth. She shut her eyes and moaned.

"Well?" Dad questioned. "What do you think?"

Heidi opened her eyes. "One word," she said. "Scrum-diddly-umptious!"

Dad sat down next to Mom at the table. "Well, move over, Willy Wonka! Dad is *in* the *house*!"

Heidi and Mom both laughed. Then Heidi noticed the empty chair beside her.

"Where's Henry?" she asked, taking a sip of milk.

"He spent the night at Dudley's, remember?" Mom said. "He'll be home later this afternoon."

Heidi flung her napkin up in the air. "Yes! Now there's no one to bug me at breakfast!" she cried. "Woo-hoo!"

Mom and Dad shook their heads. Then Mom jotted some notes into her phone.

"Heidi, I have to run some errands downtown," she said. "Would you like to come with me?"

Heidi wiped her mouth with her napkin, which had landed on the table in front of her.

"I'd love to!" she said. "Can Lucy and Bruce come too?"

Mom winked. "Already invited them," she said.

Heidi clapped her hands. "Yay!" she cried. "This is going to be the best day ever!"

Chapter 2

SHOPPERS GONNA SHOP

Heidi and her friends loved to browse in all the fun little shops on Main Street.

"Let's meet at Toasty's for lunch in an hour," Mom said. "And stay on *this* side of the street only."

Heidi nodded.

The kids raced into the first store: Bumblebee's Books. Bells jingle-jangled as they walked through the door. The floorboards creaked under their feet on their way to the children's section in the back of the store. Bruce pulled a book of jokes from one of the shelves.

"'What do you call a bear with no teeth?'" he asked.

Heidi tapped the side of her head. "Harmless?" she guessed.

Lucy giggled.

"Nope!" Bruce said. "'A GUMMY bear!' Get it?!"

The girls shrieked with laughter.

Then Bruce handed the book to Heidi.
She turned the page.

"'What do birds give out on Halloween?'"

Lucy raised her hand as if she were in school. "I know!" she said. "Gummy worms!"

"Nope, but nice try!" Heidi giggled. "'They give out TWEETS.'"

Lucy and Bruce groaned.

They shared a few more jokes and then scampered next door to Hazel's Bakery.

"Look!" Heidi cried. "Sugar cookie samples!" They tasted the broken cookie pieces. Confetti sprinkles and

crumbs speckled the floor as they munched and walked toward the door. Next they wandered into the Cheese Shop. One whiff and they ran right back out.

"Ew!" Lucy cried. "It smells like a pile of old sneakers in there!"

Heidi pinched her nose.

"Excuse me, Mr. Cheese Shop Owner," she said with her nose plugged, "may I buy a wheel of stinky old tennis shoes . . . ?"

Then they all busted out laughing
and continued down the sidewalk.
They passed Miss Harriet's Dress
Shop, where Melanie Maplethorpe
got all her foofy outfits. Then they

came to their favorite store, the Enchanted Forest—the best toy store in the whole world. It had a pirate ship, a costume chest, and funhouse mirrors.

Heidi put on crazy glasses and a feather boa, but they were too itchy! Bruce grabbed a top hat and cane. Lucy put on a pink curly wig. Then they each stood in front of a mirror.

"I'm short!" Heidi shrieked.

"I'm lo-o-o-ng and stretchy!" Lucy cried. "Like a giraffe!"

"And I'm all wavy gravy!" Bruce said, swaying from side to side.

Then they tossed their costumes back into the trunk and looked at all the toys. Heidi found a ring that had a secret compartment. Lucy found 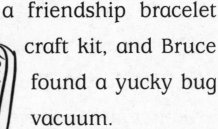 a friendship bracelet craft kit, and Bruce found a yucky bug vacuum.

"It sucks up bugs without hurting them!" Bruce said. "I wish I had invented this!"

"You could've EASILY invented that," Heidi said. "But someday you'll invent something even better."

Bruce sucked up a plastic bug and set it free.

Then they each paid for their things and ran back down the street to Toasty's. Mom had already ordered

grilled cheese sandwiches and tomato
soup for everyone.

"What did you like best about your
shopping trip?" Mom asked.

"The funhouse mirrors!" Bruce said.

"The lame jokes!" Lucy added.

"Definitely this ring," Heidi said, displaying it for her mother.

Lucy and Bruce watched her open and close the secret compartment.

"I wish every day was as awesome as today," Lucy said.

"Me too!" agreed Bruce.

"Me three!" Heidi said.

Chapter 3

A GOLD STAR DAY

"Now, who wants to go to the Brewster Arcade?" Heidi's mom suggested.

Heidi whirled and stared in shock at her mother. "The ARCADE? But you never let us go to the arcade! You said it was 'too much'!"

"It *is* too much," Mom said. "There's

too much noise and too much going on at the same time. But it's okay once in a while."

Heidi, Lucy, and Bruce raced one another to the door and yanked it

open. Electronic sound bites filled
the air.

Blip! Blip! Blip!

Ding! Ding!

Wah-wah-wah-waaahhh!

Vroom! Vroom!

"Don't you just love the sounds of arcade games?" Heidi said joyfully.

Lucy nodded. "I love the blinky lights too!"

Bruce looked around. "I like to figure out how the games are programmed."

Then her mom handed Heidi 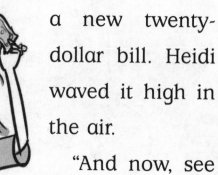 a new twenty-dollar bill. Heidi waved it high in the air.

"And now, see as I make this money magically

DISAPPEAR!" she declared. Then Heidi slipped the bill into the token machine and felt a slight tug. "Ta-da!" she cried as the tokens rained into the slot below. She gave them out.

They ran from one machine to another and played Treasure Temple, Scamper Puppies, Gotcha Ghosts, and Slithery Snakes.

"We used up
all our money!"
Heidi said.

Mom looked
at her watch.

"Then how
about a game
of glow-in-the-
dark miniature
golf?" she offered.

The kids nodded
their heads wildly.

"Could this day get any better?"
Heidi asked as she grabbed a club
and stepped onto the glow-in-the-dark

course. Everything white or neon glowed under the black lights.

"Look at my shoes!" Lucy said.

"And my golf ball!" said Bruce.

"Even my OWL is glowing!" Heidi added.

They all laughed.

Then they golfed through a castle, a shipwreck, a windmill, a barnyard, a rain forest, a haunted house, and a pyramid. Bruce won a prize for a hole in one. He picked a plastic pork chop from the prize counter.

Heidi and Lucy looked at each other and giggled.

"What?" Bruce asked as his cheeks started turning pink. "It's for my dog, Frankie."

"Oh, sure it is," Heidi said, winking at Lucy.

Then Mom said it was time to go, and they followed her to the car.

"May we have a sleepover at our house?" Heidi asked. "Please?"

Mom pressed a button, and the car beeped. "Sure!" she said, opening the door. "We can stop by Lucy's and Bruce's to get their things on our way to pick up Henry."

Heidi, Lucy, and Bruce rolled out sleeping bags in the playroom. Dad ordered pizza. Mom made popcorn. Henry lay down on the couch, and they all watched a movie.

"This is the best night EVER!" Heidi declared.

Lucy nodded. "I give it five gold stars!" she said.

Bruce yawned. "And a great big blue ribbon!" he added.

As they dragged their sleeping bags up to her room, Heidi sighed. *I wish*

EVERY day could be this much fun, she thought.

And this, of course, gave Heidi a crazy idea.

Chapter 4

HULLABALOO! HULLABALEE!

Heidi wriggled out of her sleeping bag. She pulled her *Book of Spells* and her Witches of Westwick medallion from under her bed. Then she tiptoed downstairs. The light was still on in the kitchen, so Heidi left her spell book and medallion underneath the hall table. Then she walked casually into the kitchen.

"Well, hello, pumpkin," her father greeted her. "What are you doing up?" He had a slice of apple pie on the table with a scoop of vanilla ice cream on top.

Heidi shrugged. "I'm just not sleepy, I guess."

Dad got up and gave Heidi a big bear hug.

"Did I tell you today that I love you?" he asked. Heidi shook her head against her father's shirt.

"Well, I do," he said, and he kissed her on the head. Then he pulled a second fork from the utensil drawer.

"Want to share this slice of pie with me?" he asked. Heidi sat down beside her father and they took turns having bites.

"Did you know Henry fell asleep on the couch?" Dad said, licking his fork. "I'm going to take him up. And you need to go up too."

Heidi nodded. "I will," she said. "I'm just going to put our dish in the dishwasher."

As soon as Dad was gone, Heidi grabbed her *Book of Spells* and flipped to the Contents. She found the perfect spell, called The More Things Stay the Same.

The More Things Stay the Same

Are you the kind of witch who has good days and bad days? Do you ever wish you could skip the bad days and have only good days? Would you like to take the best day you've ever had and relive it? Then this is the spell for you!

Ingredients:

The date you wish to relive

2 handfuls of all-purpose flour

1 penny

1 drop of yellow food coloring

Write the day you wish to relive
on a piece of paper and put it
in a bowl, along with the rest of
the ingredients. Stir five times.
Hold your Witches of Westwick
medallion in one hand, and
place your other hand over the
mix. Chant the following spell.

HERE IS A DAY I'D LIKE TO REPEAT.
ALL OTHER DAYS I WISH TO DELETE.
HULLABALOO! HULLABALEE!
NOW I'M AS HAPPY AS I CAN BE!

Heidi gathered all the ingredients into a bowl and cast the spell. As soon as she finished, lightning flashed and thunder rumbled overhead. *Wow,* Heidi thought. *It's thundering . . . just like it did last night before I went to bed . . . !*

RERUN

Fee-bee!

Heidi opened one eye.

FEE-bee!

Heidi opened her other eye and
peeked out her bedroom window.

I know who THAT is, Heidi said
to herself. *It's that silly chickadee*

who woke me up yesterday! My spell worked!

"Hello, little chickadee," she said. "I'm Heidi, not Phoebe—*remember*?"

The chickadee tilted its head and hopped to another branch.

Heidi pulled her covers up to her chin and breathed in. *Mmmm,* she said to herself. *It's Saturday again, and that means I get to have pumpkin muffins TWO days in a row!*

Heidi got dressed in the same outfit and did a little pose in front of the mirror. Then she bounded downstairs to the kitchen.

Dad greeted her in a blue-and-white-checked apron.

"Welcome to Dad's Diner!" he said, and set a pumpkin muffin on a tiny cupcake stand in front of her.

Heidi sat down and cut a sliver of her muffin and slid it into her mouth.

"Well, what do you think?" Dad asked.

Heidi took a sip of milk.

"It's, um, scrum-diddly-umptious!" she said, trying to remember yesterday's comment.

Dad sat down next to Mom at the table.

"Move over, Willy Wonka! Dad is *in* the *house*!"

Both of her parents laughed. Heidi laughed too, because it was weird to hear her dad say the exact same thing as yesterday.

"Where are Bruce and Lucy?" Heidi asked, taking another bite of muffin.

"Most likely at home," Mom said.
Heidi looked up from her plate.

"Oh, yea-a-a-a-ah!" she said, remembering the sleepover hadn't happened yet. "And Henry spent the night at Dudley's!"

"That's right," Mom said. Heidi watched her mother jot some notes into her phone.

"Mom, are we going downtown?" Heidi asked.

Mom nodded in disbelief. "How did you know?" she questioned.

Heidi shrugged. "Just did," she said. "Can Lucy and Bruce come too?"

Heidi already knew the answer, but she decided to play along.

Mom winked. "Already invited them," she said.

Heidi pushed back her chair. "Great," she said.

Chapter 6

MiSS KNOW-IT-ALL

"Let's meet at Toasty's for lunch in an hour. And stay on *this* side of the street only," Mom said—just like yesterday.

"Got it," Heidi said, and they headed into Bumblebee's Books. The bells jingle-jangled as before, and the floorboards creaked on the way to the

children's section too. Bruce pulled
the book of jokes from one of the
shelves.

"'What do you call a bear with no
teeth?'" he asked.

"That's so simple!"
Heidi said, knowing
the punch line. "A
GUMMY bear."

Lucy laughed
as Bruce handed
the joke book to
Heidi. She turned
the page.

"'What do birds

give out on Halloween?'" she asked.
"And FYI, it's NOT gummy worms."

Lucy and Bruce began to think, but
Heidi didn't give them a chance to
answer.

"Give up?" Heidi
asked. "'They give
out TWEETS!'"

Then she
snapped the
book shut.
"Well, this
is getting a
bit boring,"
she declared.

"You guys want to go to Hazel's Bakery?"

"Sure!" Lucy and Bruce agreed.

They walked into the bakery and up to the counter. Heidi checked out the samples.

"Oh no. Sugar cookies AGAIN!" she said. "I was kind of hoping for snickerdoodles today."

Lucy and Bruce looked at each other and shrugged. Then they tried the sugar cookies.

The next stop was the Cheese Shop.

"Let's go in!" Lucy suggested.

"P.U. No way!" Heidi said. "That place stinks to high heaven!" As Heidi waited outside on the walk way, Lucy and Bruce ran in and ran right back out.

"Ew!" exclaimed Lucy. "It smells like old sneakers in there!"

"Told you," Heidi said, skipping yesterday's joke about ordering a wheel of old tennis shoes.

Then they walked down the street to the Enchanted Forest. Like the day

before, they put on props and posed

in front of the mirrors, but Heidi

ruined the fun.

"I'm short, you're stretchy, and you're wavy gravy," Heidi said. "NEXT!"

Lucy and Bruce looked at each other and shrugged again. They decided to look at toys.

Heidi found the same ring from yesterday. She still wanted it, but it wasn't as fun as finding it the first time. Lucy and Bruce found the same stuff too.

Bruce held up the bug vacuum. "I wish I had invented this," he said a little sadly.

Heidi had no patience for hearing Bruce say the same thing a second time.

"Coulda, shoulda, woulda!" she said.

Bruce frowned.

Heidi had the same attitude at Toasty's.

"What did you like best about your shopping trip?" Mom asked.

Heidi plunked her hand in the middle of the table. "I guess this ring's pretty cool," she said.

Everyone ate the grilled cheese sandwiches, except for Heidi. She was in the mood for a PB and J, but she kept her mouth shut this time.

Lucy sighed. "I wish every day could be as awesome as today," she said.

"Me too," Bruce said.

"Hmph," said Heidi.

Then Heidi's mom offered to take them to the Brewster Arcade. This time Heidi simply held out her hand and waited for the money. Her mother placed a twenty-dollar bill in it and frowned.

"Oh, sorry," Heidi said, forgetting her manners. "Thank you, Mom." Then she put the bill into the token machine and the tokens clanked into

the slot below. Heidi gave out the coins again. Then they played the same games as yesterday, followed by a game of miniature golf.

"May we have a sleepover at our house?" Heidi asked.

Mom pulled out her car keys.

"Oh why not!" Mom said. "We can stop by Lucy's and Bruce's to get their things on our way to pick up Henry."

Heidi, Lucy, and Bruce rolled out sleeping bags in the playroom. Dad ordered pizza AGAIN. This time

Heidi only had two bites. Mom made popcorn AGAIN. This time Heidi got a piece stuck between her teeth. Henry still lay on the couch, and then— surprise, surprise!—they all watched the same movie AGAIN. And this time Heidi fell asleep.

"I would give this day FIVE gold stars," Lucy said.

"And a blue ribbon!" Bruce added.

Heidi woke up and rubbed her eyes. "Yup," she said.

Then they went up to Heidi's room. Heidi didn't feel sleepy anymore, so

she went to the kitchen. Dad told her he loved her again and offered to share his slice of apple pie.

Heidi hadn't eaten much all day, so she sat down and began to devour the pie.

"Hey!" Dad cried. "Save some for me!"

Heidi had left only two bites.

"Oops! Sorry, Dad," she said.

Then Dad polished off the pie. "Did you know Henry fell asleep on the couch?" he said, licking his fork. "I'm going to take him up. And you need to go up too."

Heidi set down her fork.

"Okay," Heidi said. "Night, Dad."

Then there was a flash of lightning and thunder rumbled overhead.

Chapter 7

GRUMP-A-SAURUS

Fee-bee!

Heidi opened her eyes and sat up.

FEE-bee!

"Oh, now be QUIET, Phoebe," she scolded. Then she pulled down the shade and flopped back down on her bed. She smelled pumpkin muffins and pulled the covers over her head. *Not again!* she thought.

At breakfast she pushed her muffin away. "Don't we have anything else to eat?" Heidi asked.

Mom looked up from her phone. "Not really," she said. "I planned to go shopping this morning."

Heidi let out a heavy sigh.

Then Mom *made* Heidi go shopping with Lucy and Bruce. This time her friends had to beg her to go to the bookstore, the bakery, *and* the Enchanted Forest.

"Why are you so grumpy today?" Lucy asked.

Heidi folded her arms and wanted to tell them everything, but she knew her friends wouldn't understand. "Oh, NEVER MIND. It's nothing," she said.

Lucy backed off. So did Bruce.

Nobody talked over lunch at Toasty's, except when Heidi had a complaint for her mom.

"Why'd you order grilled cheese sandwiches, anyway?" she asked. "You didn't even ask us what we wanted."

Mom's eyes narrowed. "Because you love grilled cheese," she said. "That's why."

Heidi knew that normally if she'd spoken to her mom like that, the playdate would have been over right then and there. But her spell was too strong, so the day continued.

At the arcade Heidi gave her coins to Lucy and Bruce. She didn't feel

like playing, so she just stood and watched this time. She didn't bother with the glow-in-the dark miniature golf game either.

"What's the matter, Heidi?" Bruce asked. "You don't seem like yourself."

Heidi looked away and tapped her foot. She felt bad that she'd spoiled the day for her friends. But they had no idea she was living the same day for the *third* time.

Suddenly she blurted out, "Maybe we should have a sleepover." Then she covered her mouth.

Her spell *was* strong! The thought of more pizza, more popcorn, and watching the same movie sounded awful.

And it was.

Chapter 8

HERE WE GO AGAIN!

This has to stop! Heidi said to herself as she kicked off her sleeping bag. *There is no WAY I'm going to relive this day again!* She raced to her room for her *Book of Spells* and medallion. Then she marched downstairs to the kitchen.

Oh, MERG! she thought. *Dad's still in the kitchen, and he's going to try to share his apple pie with me again.* She stashed her *Book of Spells* and medallion under the hall table. Then she walked into the kitchen.

"Hi, Dad. I know you really want to share that piece of pie with me," she said, trying to speed things along, "but I'm not in the mood, so please don't bother asking."

Dad chuckled and gave Heidi a great big hug, and, of course, he told her that he loved her.

"I already ate the pie," he said. "But I'll tuck you in. It's late!"

Heidi's eyes grew wide. *Oh no! I'm too late!* she thought. *There is NO TIME for tucking in! I have to reverse this spell!*

"But I thought you had to take Henry up to bed," she said, trying to act normal.

Dad shook his head. "Nope, I took him up just before you came down."

Heidi eyes darted back and forth. *That must've been the same time I was getting my spell book!*

Dad nudged Heidi toward the stairs. "Up you go!"

Heidi thumped up the stairs. *How am I going to reverse the spell when my book is downstairs?* she wondered.

Now I'm doomed to relive the SAME day all over again!

Then Henry's door creaked open, and he appeared in the hallway.

"What are you doing up, son?" Dad asked.

"I'm thirsty." He blinked sleepily.

Dad directed Heidi back to her bedroom and into her sleeping bag. Then he got Henry a glass of water.

Finally the house became quiet. Heidi snuck back downstairs, and just as she reached for her *Book of Spells,* lightning flashed and thunder rumbled overhead.

Heidi looked at the ceiling. "Oh no!" she groaned. "Here we go again!"

Chapter 9

REVERSE THE CURSE!

Fee-bee!

Heidi opened her eyes and banged on the window. "And don't come back!" she shouted at the chickadee. Then she hid under the covers.

"Make this day GO AWAY!" she shouted into her pillow. But it didn't

go away. And Heidi rebelled.

First she wore a new outfit. Then she refused to eat breakfast.

But Mom still dragged her and her friends shopping.

At lunch Heidi drowned her grilled cheese in the bottom of her soup.

Then Heidi got on her knees and made her mother promise to never take her to the arcade or to glow-in-the-dark miniature golf ever again.

At the sleepover Heidi made signs and taped them up:

Finally, when it was bedtime, Heidi ditched her sleeping bag, zoomed downstairs, and burst into the kitchen.

"Dad, I have a HUGE confession to make!" she blurted out.

Dad laid his reading glasses on the table and pushed his apple pie to the side.

"What's the matter, Heidi?" he asked, a little concerned.

Then Heidi told her father about the spell she had cast so she could relive the perfect day and how she had now lived it FOUR times.

"Please, Dad," Heidi begged. "You HAVE to help me. I can't go through it again!" A tear rolled down her cheek.

Dad shook his head and rested his hand on his forehead.

"Can you reverse the spell?" he asked.

Heidi nodded. "But I may not have enough time before it starts up all over again," she cried.

Dad got up from the table.

"Come on," he said. "Let's get started."

Heidi pulled out her *Book of Spells* and medallion.

Dad got out a bowl and a mixing spoon. Heidi opened her book to the spell she had cast the other day. On the next page, there was a spell called The More Things Change.

The More Things Change

Are you the kind of witch who tried the spell to relive the perfect day? Do you now long to go back to having a variety of days? Perhaps you'd even like to take the best day you've ever had and forget it forever? If so, then this is the spell for you!

Ingredients:

1 calendar of all the days of the year

2 handfuls of all-purpose flour

A quarter

A drop of blue food coloring

Combine all the ingredients in one bowl. Hold your Witches of Westwick medallion in one hand, and place your other hand over the mix. Chant the following spell.

HAVE YOU RELIVED THE PERFECT DAY?
THEN WHAT a PRICE YOU HAD TO PAY!
NOW TAKE AWAY
THE DREAD AND FEAR,
RESTORE ALL DAYS
THROUGHOUT THE YEAR!

Heidi and Dad gathered all the
ingredients and created a mix. Then
Heidi held her medallion and reversed
the spell.

As soon as she finished chanting,
there was a flash of lightning and
thunder rumbled overhead.

"Oh no!" Heidi wailed. "I didn't do
it in time!

Chapter 10

BURNT TOAST

In the morning Heidi woke up to the tappity-tap of rain on the roof. She sat up in bed. The house smelled like stinky burnt toast. Heidi threw back the covers and ran downstairs in her pj's and bare feet.

The kitchen was super-smoky.

"Good morning, sunshine," Dad said. "I burned breakfast."

The fan was on and the back door was wide open even though it was raining. Heidi threw her arms around her father.

"Thank you, Dad!" she cried. "That's the best news I've heard all week!"

Dad laughed. "Then you must've had a very tough week!" he said.

Heidi danced around the kitchen. "You have no idea!" she said. Then Heidi stopped and looked at her father in the eyes. "Or do you?" Dad fanned the smoke with a magazine. He didn't say anything about their special spell.

"Are Lucy and Bruce still here?" Heidi asked.

Mom set down her coffee cup.

"How could they still be here if they weren't here at all?" she questioned.

Heidi squealed and kissed her mother. "And is Henry still at Dudley's?" she asked.

Mom nodded. "And today is still Saturday, in case you forgot."

Heidi pranced to the back door.

"But this is a BRAND-NEW, never-ever-happened-before Saturday!" she called to the outdoors.

"It's a shame that it's raining, though," said Mom. "I was going to surprise you with a shopping day. Will you take a rain check?"

Then Heidi skipped back into the kitchen. "Absolutely! Hey, maybe we could go out for breakfast?"

Dad opened a window. "Great
idea," he said. "The house needs to
air out, and I have to pick up an apple
pie anyway."

Mom smiled and went to get her
coat.

"Can we pick up cider doughnuts instead of apple pie?" Heidi asked.

Dad untied his apron. "Sure, why not!" he said.

Then Heidi got dressed and had a brand-new, never-ever-happened-before day.

And it was perfect.

Check out the next book starring

HEIDI HECKELBECK

"Ha-a-a hu-u-um," Heidi yawned.

She rubbed her eyes and padded across the kitchen in her bunny slippers and pink polka-dot pajamas. Heidi loved to have breakfast in her pj's on Sunday morning. But she didn't love it when Henry acted like an unexpected alarm clock.

An excerpt from Heidi Heckelbeck Has a New Best Friend

"GUESS WHAT!" Henry yelled as he walked in the back door.

Heidi was so surprised, she spilled her milk.

Henry didn't even make fun of her, so the whole family knew he must have big news. "We have NEW NEIGHBORS!"

Heidi wiped up the mess. "We do?"

Henry nodded proudly. "Yep. There's a moving truck and everything. RIGHT. NEXT. DOOR."

Heidi's bunny slippers hopped across the floor as she ran to the window to see.

An excerpt from *Heidi Heckelbeck Has a New Best Friend*

"You're right!" she cried.

"TOLD YOU!" Henry said. "I've been spying on them ever since I got up."

Mom set her teacup on her saucer. "HENRY!" she scolded. "It's not polite to spy."

Henry shrugged. "But, Mom, how else am I going to find out important stuff, like that they have a GIANT trampoline?"

Mom frowned. "Nobody likes a snoop, young man."

An excerpt from *Heidi Heckelbeck Has a New Best Friend*